izzy's place

Also by Marc Kornblatt

Understanding Buddy

(Margaret K. McElderry Books)

izzy's place

MARC KORNBLATT

MARGARET K. McELDERRY BOOKS
New York   London   Toronto   Sydney   Singapore

Margaret K. McElderry Books
An imprint of Simon & Schuster
Children's Publishing Division
1230 Avenue of the Americas,
New York, New York 10020

Book design by Ann Sullivan
The text for this book is set in Stempel Garamond.

Printed in the United States of America
2 4 6 8 10 9 7 5 3 1
Library of Congress Cataloging-in-Publication Data
Kornblatt, Marc.
Izzy's place / Marc Kornblatt.
p. cm.
Summary: While spending the summer at his grandmother's Indiana home,
ten-year-old Henry Stone gets help from a new friend in coping
with the recent death of his grandfather and the possibility of
his parents getting divorced.
ISBN 0-689-84639-8
[1. Family problems—Fiction. 2. Death—Fiction. 3. Grandparents—
Fiction. 4. Indiana—Fiction.] I. Title.
PZ7.K8373 Iz 2003
[Fic]—dc21
2002006185

For Judith

With thanks to Emma

izzy's place

1

A LONG ROW OF BRIGHTLY COLORED FLAGS GREETED Henry Stone as he entered the Indianapolis airport terminal. Drooping one after another like giant, silent birds, the flags reminded him of the United Nations. Except he knew the U.N. was back in New York City.

"Yoo-hoo, Henry!"

Grandma Martha waved to him from behind a metal rail, holding a yellow balloon in her other hand. Henry glimpsed a smiley face printed on one side of it, knowing it was meant for him, wishing it weren't.

Brother! He had just finished fourth grade. Didn't his own grandmother know that he was too old for smiley face balloons?

"I'm so glad to see you," she cried, hugging him so tightly that he could smell her hair spray and lemon-scented perfume. "How was your trip, honey?"

"Okay." Henry untangled himself from her smothering embrace and tightened one of the straps on his backpack to hide his embarrassment.

"Not too lonely?"

"Nah."

"Are you sure?"

"I'm sure."

Henry wished Grandma Martha would stop trying so hard; she was making him tired.

She brushed back a wisp of brown hair that had strayed into his eyes. "My goodness, you're getting so big."

It was something she said every time they met. Grandmother talk.

"Pretty soon I'll be taller than you are." Henry played along.

"Yes, you will."

Shaped like a teapot, Grandma Martha was only a head taller than Henry now and slowly shrinking, while he, though small for his age, had grown two inches since last Thanksgiving and looked more and more like his grandpa, who had always been slim and straight as a saltshaker.

Leaning down so she could look him in the eye, his grandmother quietly asked, "How are you, Henry?"

"Okay," he said, which wasn't really true. But it was the best answer he could come up with in the middle of an airport.

Grandma Martha sighed sympathetically, then held out the balloon.

"Welcome to Indiana, sweetheart."

"Thanks." Henry refused to smile as he took the balloon. If only he had a pin.

They headed down a crowded corridor lined with more drooping flags. If Grandpa Jay were there, he would have made a game out of finding England's Union Jack and the maple leaf of Canada. But he wasn't. Henry's favorite grandparent was gone. Gone forever. Henry hung his head like one of the flags and trudged on.

An escalator carried them downstairs to the first floor. As soon as they stepped onto solid ground Grandma Martha reached for Henry's hand.

"Let's hold on to each other so we don't get separated," she said.

"But you just told me how big I am," Henry protested.

"Henry, take my hand and don't argue with me."

Slowly, they made their way through the crowd.

Henry could hear his dad's voice back at Newark airport. "Promise me you'll be easy on your grandma," he had said. "She's had a tough year."

Henry had promised, but he hadn't expected to be treated like a first grader as soon as he got off the plane. He wished his dad were there to see. Surely, he would understand.

His mom had tucked a note into his shirt pocket when she hugged him good-bye. "Read it on the plane," she had whispered. The note was a poem.

Rose are red,
Violets are blue,
Wherever I am,
I'll think often of you.
Roses are red,
Violets are gray,
I hope you and Grandma
Have fun every day.

Who ever heard of gray violets? They were supposed to be blue, weren't they? But the color his mother chose seemed right, considering how things felt. Folding the paper in half again and again until it was the size of his pinky, Henry had dropped the poem into the bottom of his backpack and tried to forget about it as he stared out the plane window at clouds shaped like dragons.

He studied his grandmother out of the corner of his eye. She reminded him of a little steam engine, the way she chugged along, her puffy white hair billowing atop her head like smoke.

"Keep your eyes open for Area D," she instructed, still clutching his hand.

"You're squeezing my fingers."

"I don't want to lose you."

"My hand is getting numb!"

"Is it really?"

Grandma Martha loosened her grip slightly.

Henry knew she meant well and that he should listen to her. *But has she forgotten everything she learned as a mother,* he wondered, *or has she always been like this?* Either way, Henry didn't feel like holding hands. When he saw a sign with a big *D* on it, he pulled out of her grasp.

"There's our area, Grandma!"

"Henry!"

As he sped toward the luggage carousel Henry let the smiley face balloon string slip through his fingers.

2

It was a hot, humid June day. The air conditioner in Grandma Martha's old blue station wagon was broken, so they rolled down all the windows and drove along the highway with the air blowing in their faces. The wind made it too noisy to talk, which was just as well.

After catching up with Henry at the baggage claim area, Grandma Martha had grabbed him roughly by the arm. "Henry, how could you run away from me like that?"

"I didn't run away."

"I told you to stay close, didn't I?" She was practically crying. "Didn't I?"

"Yes."

Passersby had stared as Grandma Martha stood hugging Henry so close, he could barely breathe. He wished he could have run all the way back to New Jersey. Not to the home that was there now, of course, but to the one he lived in when life was still good and his parents hardly ever argued.

The highway took them past farmhouses flanked by shade trees, cows grazing in meadows, and field after field after boring field of ankle-high corn. The only relief from the monotony was a faded road sign advertising BIG CHUCK'S CHEWING TOBACCO. The painting of the baseball player on the sign was pretty good, but the idea of chewing a wad of tobacco made Henry feel like throwing up.

If only he had a remote control clicker that would let him change the date and the scenery. *Click.* Henry would jump back one year to his friend Ben Gellman's tree house where the two of them had spent hours and hours battling Dr. Evil and his army of dweebs. *Click.* He would jump back to the first day of fourth grade, when his mom and dad had stood together like friends, waving to him from the sidewalk as his bus pulled away. *Click.* He would jump back to Grandpa Jay yanking a banana out of his nose or singing him his favorite goofy song.

> *I went downtown to see my girl,*
> *My shoes they were a squeakin'.*
> *Her mouth I missed,*
> *Her nose I kissed,*
> *And found the darn thing leakin'!*

Click. Click. Click. Click.

Henry could think of a hundred places and times he would jump to rather than be stuck here in Indiana alone with Grandma Martha. But magic clickers were found only in movies and books. In real life Ben and his family were driving out West to camp in the Badlands, Henry's parents weren't friends anymore, and Grandpa Jay was dead. Henry felt like screaming.

"You need to be with your grandma," was how his mom had explained things earlier that week.

"Why?" asked Henry.

"Because the way things are at home now, your dad and I think you'll have a better summer with her than with us."

"Why?"

"Because it will be more peaceful for you."

"But I don't want to go."

"We understand," said his dad. "But we want you to—for your own good."

"And for Grandma Martha, too," added his mom. "She could really use some company."

Henry had let the matter drop. His going to Grandma Martha's was one of the few things his parents had agreed about in months. And he had to agree too. It would be more peaceful with her than with them.

His mom had been living in the basement guest room since the winter, but that hadn't helped. Whenever she and Henry's dad were together, there was trouble. They fought about who was busier and who should pick up Henry at After-School Club. They fought about the phone bill and the grocery shopping and about the laundry and the snow shoveling. And about how high to set the thermostat. The fight over Grandma Bessie and Pappa Sam's coffee cups had been one of the worst.

When Grandma Bessie and Pappa Sam died, Henry's dad had inherited their good china. There were eight place settings, complete with large main course plates, cups and saucers and dessert dishes, all of them decorated with fancy pink and purple flowers. When he was in second grade, Henry couldn't understand how china could come from Czechoslovakia. Once he learned the difference between a capital *C* and a lowercase *c*, his earlier confusion became a family joke. Whenever they used the place settings for a special occasion, he or one of his parents would always ask, "How can china come from Czechoslovakia?" and the three of them would laugh.

Soon after Mr. Kahn sold his share of the rug store to Henry's dad, the good china stopped being funny. It felt so long ago, but Henry knew it was only a year last spring. Since then, Henry's dad had been spending more and more time in the store and had grown grumpier and grumpier. His mom, too. Between her job, college classes, and her homework, she always had something else on her mind and would run out of patience in the blink of an eye.

Henry didn't even have time to blink the night his dad came home late from work and found Henry and his mom drinking hot chocolate out of two of the good china cups.

"Those are only for special occasions," he said, his voice tight.

"Isn't Henry's bedtime special enough?" his mom asked, scowling.

Just like that, his parents began yelling at each other. His dad banged the kitchen table so hard that one of the cups fell to the floor, smashing into jagged pieces. And his parents still kept on yelling at each other. Henry ran up to his room and hid his head under his pillow, humming as loudly as he could so he wouldn't have to hear them.

He had hidden his head under his pillow a lot since

his mother had moved into the guest room. But sometimes, when their shouting got so loud that his pillow and humming didn't help, Henry had to scream to drown out his parents' voices. And once he started screaming, he didn't know how to stop. Even if his mom or dad tried to hug him, he couldn't stop. Henry would scream and scream and scream until there was no air left in his lungs. Then he would fall asleep.

His parents sent him to a child psychologist to talk about his screaming. Dr. Cohen told Henry he had every right to scream, that he would probably scream too if his mother and father were always fighting. Dr. Cohen was the one who had advised his parents to see a marriage counselor. He also had suggested that Henry go away for the summer to get a break from all of their fighting. The fact that Grandma Martha was so lonely without Grandpa Jay, and that Henry's parents thought he was too young for overnight camp, made Greenville, Indiana, the most suitable place for his vacation.

"You're going to have all kinds of fun out there," Henry remembered his mom telling him as she'd said good-bye at the airport. "The air is much cleaner than it is in New Jersey, and your grandma will be delighted to have you."

Oh, sure, Henry told himself now. *I'll bet she's already sorry I'm here.*

Fed up with the view out the car window, he unzipped his backpack and took out a slim book his father had given him as a going-away present. He turned to the first page. "Juggling is a hobby you can take anywhere," it read. "You don't need a partner to do it, just time and persistence."

His dad had also given him three orange beanbags with which to practice. Henry liked the gifts. He intended to impress his dad with his juggling when he got home.

His mom had given him the poem about the gray violets and a box of fancy stationery. "I hope you'll write often," she had said.

"Henry, look!"

Grandma Martha pointed to a sign on the road that read, GREENVILLE 4 MI.

She turned around for a moment and caught Henry's eye. "We're almost there."

Henry knew that Grandpa Jay would have had him figuring out how many feet were in four miles or maybe started singing some goofy made-up song about driving down the highway with his wife, his grandson, and two flat tires.

Grandma smiled in a shy kind of way. "We're almost there," she repeated, as if she knew what Henry was thinking.

She was trying her best. Henry regretted letting

go of the balloon. Grandma Martha hadn't said anything about it.

They slowed down and turned off the highway.
Now that the wind wasn't blowing so hard, it was
possible to talk. Henry flipped through the pages of
his juggling book, waiting for an opportunity.

"Sorry I ran away," he managed to say finally.

"Forgiven," Grandma Martha quickly replied.
"I'm sorry I grabbed you like that."

"Forgiven," said Henry.

"We all make mistakes, right?"

"Yeah."

"And I have another apology to make too."

"What?"

Grandma Martha paused, then said, "I couldn't
get you into the YMCA day camp. They were all
filled up by the time I called."

"Oh."

Henry felt like yelling. *Now what am I going to
do all summer?*

"Don't you worry," said his grandmother.
"Whenever I can, I'll close the jewelry store early and
we'll do something fun."

"Great." Henry didn't even try to smile.

Grandpa Jay had always been the one to take
Henry fishing or play cards with him. Grandma
Martha mainly worked in their jewelry store and

cooked the meals. Henry couldn't imagine searching for salamanders in the park after it rained or crawling through Wolf Cave with her. As far as he was concerned, Grandma Martha was mostly a stranger.

"Great," he repeated quietly. "Everything is going to be just great."

3

GREENVILLE SEEMED EVEN SMALLER THAN HENRY remembered. On Main Street there was the post office; Nelson's Hardware; Madge and Lyn's Clip 'n' Curl Carnival; the Greenville Consolidated Bank; the Greenville Public Library; the Big Ten Pub; Ott's Drugs; his grandparents' jewelry store, Steele's Gem Shop; and a Piggly Wiggly supermarket. That was all. There was no movie theater, no video store, not even a bowling alley. Nothing.

A wrinkly old man wearing a straw hat and overalls was sunning himself on a bench in front of the drugstore like a drowsy tortoise. Grandma Martha slowed down and tooted her horn at him.

"Watch out you don't get sunstroke, Tobias," she called.

"Yes, dear," the man replied. "Certainly is."

Grandma Martha stopped the car.

"Tobias," she practically shouted. "I said, watch out that you don't get sunstroke."

"My son's fine," he replied. "Got a call from Calvin day before yesterday. Boy's up for promotion at John Deere."

Grandma Martha pointed to her ear. "Tobias Sweet, turn on your hearing aid!"

The man nodded and fiddled with a crescent-shaped device behind his left ear.

"Sorry, Martha," he said. "Forgot I shut it off. Thing was buzzin' so much, it was drivin' me crazy."

"How long have you been sitting there?" asked Grandma Martha.

"I finished lunch around eleven forty-five." Tobias Sweet checked his wristwatch. "Two hours, give or take."

"Do you want a ride home?"

"No, thank you, dear. The exercise does an old geezer like me good."

"Make sure you drink something, or you'll get dehydrated."

"Ethel will have lemonade waitin'. You want to come over for a cold glass?"

"It sounds inviting, but I want to take my grandson home. He's been traveling all day."

Tobias Sweet shuffled toward the car. Catching sight of Henry, he waved.

"Hello there, young fella. I've forgotten your name."

"It's Henry."

"You look like the spittin' image of your grandpa Jay. Knew him his whole life. One of the finest men I ever met."

"Kind of you to say that, Tobias," said Grandma Martha.

"It's the truth. Great sense of humor. Used to love to hear him sing that salty song about Barnacle Bill the sailor." He cleared his throat and bellowed, "Who's that knockin' at my door? Who's that knockin' at my door? Who's that—"

"Tell Ethel I said hello," said Grandma Martha, interrupting him.

"Indeed I will."

The old man nodded for what seemed like half an hour before he shuffled back to his bench. As Grandma Martha picked up speed Henry wished he had a hearing aid so he could switch off all boring conversations. And arguments.

Turning right after the Piggly Wiggly, they were headed down Lincoln Street when something struck the car's back window.

Splat!

"What on earth?"

The wheels screeched as Grandma Martha pulled over to the curb. Henry jumped out of the car. A splotch of yellow slime flecked with little white chips oozed down the window.

"Was it a bird?" she asked.

"No," said Henry. "An egg."

He spotted a lanky boy running down Main Street, but by the time Grandma Martha turned the car around and headed back in that direction, the boy had disappeared.

"For shame," Grandma Martha muttered. "For shame!"

Down at the police station the young officer in charge was very patient, but Henry was unable to give him any specific details besides the fact that the alleged egg hurler was probably a teenager.

"Did you see his face, son?" the police officer asked.

"No," said Henry.

"What was he wearing?"

"A shirt. Blue jeans, I think."

"What color was his shirt?"

"I don't remember."

"Well, I'm afraid that doesn't give us much to go on."

"George," said Grandma Martha, "don't you have a list of usual suspects?"

"Not for a prank like this, Mrs. Steele. But we'll follow up."

"I should hope so. That boy's parents should be ashamed!"

Grandma Martha was upset by the incident, but for Henry, the trip to the police station was the highlight of his day. It reminded him of the time he and his dad saw a woman fall on the sidewalk near home. His dad had stopped the car, and they ran across the street to see if she was okay. She told them she thought she had broken her hip, and they called 911 on his dad's cell phone. Two police cars and an ambulance got to the scene within minutes. Henry had felt very important staying by the woman's side until the paramedics lifted her into the waiting ambulance and took her to the hospital. His dad had been proud of him. Later, when they told his mother, she had called Henry the bravest boy she knew and kissed him on both cheeks, like they do in France. Henry was only seven at the time, but he could remember the whole thing like it had happened yesterday.

The visit to the police station with Grandma was not that special, of course, and it was over in twenty minutes. By the time they got back into the car, the broken egg had dried to a faint yellow memory on the glass.

Grandma Martha's neighborhood was even less exceptional than Main Street. It seemed all but

deserted. Henry didn't see another boy his age anywhere. As they pulled in front of the clean white
house at the corner of Lincoln and Garfield Streets,
he remembered playing gin rummy on the screened-
in porch with Grandpa Jay. What Henry liked best
about playing cards with Grandpa Jay was that his
grandfather never let him win just because he was a
kid. He taught Henry the rules, and they played for
real while Grandpa Jay smoked his pipe and Henry
had apple cider or milk and cookies.

"Make no mistake about it, Henry, my boy," he
could hear his grandfather say in his fake gangster
voice. "When I play cards, I take no prisoners."

"Same here," Henry would banter back.

"Then let's get to it!"

Henry didn't think Grandma Martha even knew
how to play Go Fish.

"Home sweet home," she said, switching off the
ignition. "Finally." She gave a half smile and added,
"It's nice to have you here, honey."

"Thanks." Henry got out of the car quickly, just
in case she wanted to hug him again.

In the yard next door a heavyset man wearing a
blue baseball cap crouched beside a lawn mower, filling it with gas from a red metal canister. Henry had
seen the man from a distance a few times over the
years, but he couldn't recall his name. Grandpa Jay
had always taken up most of Henry's attention dur-

ing his visits. His grandfather had said that the neighbors were both teachers who liked to travel, but that was about all Henry could remember.

The man was a good deal older than Henry's father, old enough to maybe be a grandfather himself. As soon as he saw Grandma Martha, he removed his cap, which had a big C on the front of it, and stood up slowly.

"Hello, Martha," he said in a voice as deep as a bass drum. "How are you today?"

"Good, thanks. Except for a run-in we had with a prankster."

"What happened?"

"Somebody threw an egg at our window."

Observing his grandmother's neighbor up close for the first time, Henry was amazed by his size. He recalled that the man was big, but he'd never realized just how big he was. He not only towered over Henry and his grandmother like a giant sloth next to two squirrels, but everything about him seemed huge. His head, ears, and lips looked as though they had been inflated to the bursting point with an air pump. His arms and legs looked like logs, his work boots like canoes. They had to be size 15, at least.

"Did you catch the person?" asked the giant, looking straight at Henry.

Henry shrank back.

"No," he managed to say. "But we filed a report with the police."

"That was wise." The man kept his gaze on Henry.

"Ernie, this is my grandson Henry, Judith's boy," said Grandma Martha. "I'm sure you two have met before."

"Yes, in passing." The man's smile flashed like a spark in the night, then died. "Welcome back to town, Henry," he said, reaching out his hand. "The full name is Ernie Fine, for the record."

"Nice to meet you."

The sloth's huge paw swallowed up Henry's fingers as they shook hands. Mr. Fine studied Henry in silence before letting go. Henry was relieved to get his hand back unbroken.

Grandma Martha put her arm around Henry's shoulder and squeezed him as though trying to keep him warm.

"Henry's come to stay with me for the summer," she said.

"You must be pleased," said Mr. Fine.

"I'm delighted. How is Louise today?"

Mr. Fine shrugged. "Hanging in there."

"Do you two need anything?"

"No. Thanks."

"Tell her I said hello."

"Will do."

After putting on his hat, Mr. Fine picked up the gas canister, then rolled the lawn mower a few feet before he stopped and walked back to Henry.

"You're from New Jersey?" he asked.

"Yes," replied Henry.

"Ever visit New York City?"

"Of course."

"Great place." Mr. Fine gazed up at the sky. "We've got a building on Main Street with more stories than the Empire State Building."

"I don't believe it."

"It's a fact." Mr. Fine stared at the sky again. "Our library has more stories in it than any skyscraper in the world."

Without waiting for a response, he turned back to his lawn mower and slowly pushed it down the alley. Henry thought it was a dumb pun, but when he looked at his grandmother, she was smiling.

"You must be a good influence."

"Why?"

"That's the first joke I've heard Ernie Fine tell in I don't know how long." Grandma Martha watched him head down the alley with the mower. "The man used to have a sense of humor, like Grandpa Jay."

"What happened to him?" asked Henry.

"His world is . . ." Grandma Martha paused before she quietly added, "falling apart."

"How?"

"The same way mine did."

Henry carried his suitcase up the front steps with

his grandmother's help, then rolled it through the tidy living room over the pale yellow carpet. Grandpa Jay's green velvet easy chair still stood alongside Grandma Martha's rocker, just as it always had, in front of the television. His pipe still rested on the mantel above the fireplace beside a pack of playing cards with pictures of American songbirds on the backs. The aroma of sweet cherry tobacco still hung faintly in the air. But the room seemed much quieter than Henry remembered it. Grandma Martha paused to fluff up the pillow on the green easy chair.

"I'm sorry your grandfather isn't here to keep us company," she said.

Henry sighed. "Me too."

"But you still have me, and I still have you." His grandmother kissed the top of his head. "And he loved both of us very much. We have to remember that. Right?"

"Right."

The stairs squeaked as they made their way up to his mom's old room. It would be Henry's for the summer. As they set the suitcase on the bed they heard a lawn mower roar to life.

Gazing out the window, Henry saw Mr. Fine cutting the grass in the backyard next door. Grandma Martha looked too. Together, they watched Mr. Fine push the lawn mower like someone in a slow-motion movie.

"He's having a hard, hard time," she said.

"Why?"

Grandma Martha held her eyes on her neighbor for a long while before she turned to Henry.

"His wife Louise is very ill."

Grandma Martha brushed a strand of hair from Henry's forehead, then hugged him close as the lawn mower's moaning cleaved the air.

4

"HI, CHAMP. HOW'D THE FLIGHT GO?"

"Okay."

Henry's dad was talking in his chipper voice, the one that made him sound like a businessman.

"How's your grandma?"

"Okay." Henry twirled the phone cord around his fingers.

"What have you two been up to?"

"We unpacked my suitcase. Ate dinner. Now we're watching TV."

"What's on?"

"Reruns."

"Sounds like you're doing fine," said his dad.

"I sure am," Henry replied, meeting chipper with chipper. "Everything is great!"

"That's great," said his dad, acting even more chipper. "Did Grandma enroll you in camp?"

"No, they were all filled up."

His dad sighed. "Sorry to hear it," he said, suddenly sounding like a father.

"Did you and Mom fight on the way back from the airport?"

"No, we were both on our best behavior."

"Maybe if you stay on your best behavior, I can come home sooner."

His dad didn't answer.

"Dad?"

"We didn't send you to Greenville just because your mom and I have been fighting. We sent you to be with your grandma, too."

"I know. But the fighting was a big part of the reason, wasn't it?"

"Yes."

"Are you and Mom getting a divorce?"

"I don't know."

"Does that mean you might?"

Henry's dad didn't answer again.

"Does it?" Henry felt tears well up in the corners of his eyes.

"Look, champ," said his dad. "Everything will

be all right, okay? Don't worry."

Henry didn't answer. If everything was going to be all right, why did his dad sound so uncertain? The thought made the tears flow down his cheeks.

"Okay, champ?"

"Okay, what?"

"Hang in there."

Again, Henry didn't answer.

"I miss you, Henry."

"I miss you, too."

"I've got some work to finish up here in the store. I'll call you later in the week. Okay?"

"Okay."

"Tell your grandma I said hi."

Wiping his eyes, Henry hung up and returned to the living room, but he didn't tell his grandmother anything. She was asleep in her rocker.

5

On Sunday, Grandma Martha took Henry to church. Back home in Metuchen he rarely attended religious services. That was because his father, who was Jewish, chose to work on Saturdays rather than go to synagogue, and on Sundays his mom preferred to go with Henry on a hike or a bike ride. "My church is nature," she liked to say, a line she learned from Grandpa Jay.

The few times Henry had visited a synagogue with his father, he had liked the calm orderliness of the service and the singing, even when he didn't understand most of what was going on. And while he enjoyed Sundays outdoors with his mother, Henry was also comfortable praying inside an actual chapel.

Grandma Martha's Methodist Church services were easy to follow, especially when Pastor Williams read from the Book of Psalms. "'I waited patiently for the Lord; and He leaned toward me, and heard me cry,'" he read. "'And He put a new song in my mouth.'"

Henry wondered if God had heard him crying over his parents and if he would ever have a new song to sing. The pastor said everyone's cry would eventually be heard, but Henry wasn't sure how patient he could be.

After the service Pastor Williams welcomed Henry to town and told Grandma Martha she must be proud to have such a well-behaved youngster by her side during prayers. She nodded proudly and gave Henry one of her grandmother smiles.

On the way down the center aisle Grandma Martha stopped to talk to Tobias Sweet, who was relaxing in his pew, just like he did on the bench outside the drugstore.

"Good morning, Tobias," she said. "Where is Ethel today?"

"Yes, dear," said Mr. Sweet. "God's love is better than wealth."

Grandma Martha patted his shoulder.

"His hearing aid must be off," she told Henry.

Mr. Sweet yawned. "You have a good year too," he said.

Madge and Lyn Grackle, the identical twins who owned Madge and Lyn's Clip 'n' Curl Carnival, made a fuss over Henry.

"It's nice to have such a handsome young man staying in town for the summer," said Madge.

"Yes," agreed Lyn. "A most welcome addition."

The sisters nodded energetically to each other. They reminded Henry of two frisky golden retrievers, with their thick, blond hair and long noses.

"I adore those dimples," gushed Madge. Henry stepped back before she could squeeze his cheeks.

"Martha, we're having a twenty-fifth anniversary celebration at the shop next week," said Lynn. "Make sure you and Henry stop by for some cake."

"It will be our pleasure," said Grandma Martha.

"Styles and cuts will be half price," said Madge, appraising Henry like a painting.

"I don't need a haircut," said Henry.

"Looks to me like a trim wouldn't hurt." Madge swept an imaginary hair clipper through the air. "In case you haven't heard," she said, "I give the best buzz cuts in town."

"Of course, she's the only one who does them in town," added Lyn, and they both laughed.

Grandma Martha rescued Henry from the conversation by introducing him to Hildegaard Mollenhoffer, a bright-eyed woman whose wide, round face resembled a sunflower.

"What a nice little boy," said Mrs. Mollenhoffer, leaning over him. "Are you enjoying your stay with your grandma?"

"Actually, I'm not a little boy," Henry informed her. "I'm starting fifth grade in September."

"Is that so?" Mrs. Mollenhoffer's eyebrows rippled up and down like two amused caterpillars. "Pretty soon, people will be addressing you as 'sir.'"

She and Grandma Martha traded knowing smiles.

"I have a grandson just your age," Mrs. Mollenhoffer continued. "Maybe we can get you boys together for some fun."

Henry held his breath and counted to ten before excusing himself. On the front steps of the church he almost tripped over a lanky teenager sitting alone smoking a cigarette.

"What are you staring at?" the older boy demanded.

"Nothing," said Henry.

"Then bug off."

Henry held his ground, trying to think of something smart to say, but when the stranger shifted his legs as if he was preparing to spring, Henry retreated to his grandmother's car and waited there until she was ready to go home.

Grandma Martha wanted to save room for Sunday dinner. They were going to have roast turkey, mashed potatoes, peas, and homemade raspberry pie. So they ate a light lunch of grilled cheese sandwiches and pickles. Then Grandma Martha gave Henry some oatmeal cookies and told him to go out and play while she prepared dinner.

"Please stay in the backyard, honey," she said.

"Why?"

"I don't want you wandering off and getting lost."

"How can I get lost? I went all around Greenville a hundred times with Grandpa Jay."

"Maybe so, but for now, I'd like to keep you close by."

"Why?

"Because you've never been here alone with just me."

"So?"

"I need to know you're safe."

"But I will be safe."

"Henry, please. I want you to stay in the back-yard. And that's final."

Henry stomped upstairs to grab his beanbags, then stomped even harder downstairs and slammed the kitchen door behind him. Once outside, he threw his beanbags on the ground and kicked one. It sailed over the chain-link fence that surrounded the yard and landed in the alley between his grandparents' house and the Fines'.

He scanned the area, hungry to see something worth looking at. In the middle of the yard sat the old wooden sandbox he used to play in with Grandpa Jay when he was little. He couldn't count all of the sand castles they had built together, all the tunnels they had dug. His favorite creations were the sand dunes they had made that reached as high as Henry's belly button. Grandpa Jay would hook up an extension cord and carry an electric fan with black metal blades as big as boat propellers from the house and set it up beside the sandbox.

"Look out! A powerful sandstorm is a-comin'," he would yell. "Take cover!" Then he would turn on the gigantic fan and blow the dunes to smithereens.

Now the sandbox was full of weeds, and one of its sides had begun to rot. Not that Henry was interested in playing in it, of course.

On the right side of the yard lay Garfield Street, bland and empty as usual. On the left side grew a wall of low juniper bushes along the fence, with a gap that framed a gate opening on to the alley. Beyond the alley stood the Fines' house.

The only interesting thing now in the whole yard was a wooden swing that dangled like a fishing lure from one of the lower branches of a giant sycamore tree. Grandpa Jay had put it up when Henry's mom was a girl. The swing seat, a splintery board threaded through the middle with a thick rope, had been a few inches too high for Henry at Thanksgiving when he last visited. He had needed Grandpa Jay to help him get on.

"You're growing up, my boy," he could hear his grandfather coaxing as he had helped him onto the seat. "You're almost there."

He could almost feel the little puff of air tickle his ear as Grandpa Jay whispered, "Almost there."

Henry now grabbed the stiff rope and lifted his right leg over the seat. It was surprisingly easy. The moment he rested his thigh on the board, however, it tipped to one side and dumped him off.

His bottom hit the ground with a hard thud.

"Grandpa!" he cried.

But Grandpa Jay, of course, was nowhere near. Tears sprang to Henry's eyes.

"You okay?" asked a deep voice.

Henry looked around quickly. Mr. Fine stood by the gap in the bushes. Henry felt his cheeks burn.

"So?" said Mr. Fine. "Are you or aren't you?"

"I'm fine," said Henry, picking himself up.

"No, I'm Fine. You're Stone." Without waiting to see if Henry would smile at his joke, Mr. Fine held up the stray beanbag. "I believe this is yours."

A flip of the man's massive wrist sent the beanbag sailing over the fence. It fell inches from Henry's feet.

"Thanks," said Henry.

Mr. Fine nodded, then hesitated for a moment. He seemed about to say something else but was distracted by the sound of a screen door opening.

"Ernie," a voice called, "are you finished weeding?"

"Yes, dear."

"The Cubs' game is on."

"All right."

Henry edged closer to the fence so he could see the neighbors' house better. Mrs. Fine leaned against the back screen door as still as a statue. The sight of her gave Henry a start. He remembered her as a plump, penguin-shaped woman. Now she was thinner than a flamingo, and her skin looked gray. Seeing Henry, she smiled.

"Hello," she said in a surprisingly strong voice. "You're Martha's grandson, aren't you?"

"Yes."

"Henry," Mr. Fine offered.

"I remember." She raised her hand as though it hurt and waved.

Henry waved back.

"How are you doing, Henry?"

Mrs. Fine's inviting smile made Henry want to tell her the truth, but he was afraid if he told her just how miserable he felt that he would start crying. Instead, he answered with a shrug.

"I see," she said kindly. "Would you like to come

inside to drink lemonade and watch the Cubs?"

Henry looked to see what Mr. Fine thought of the invitation but could find no welcome in his expression.

"I can't," he said. "I need to practice my juggling."

Mrs. Fine closed her eyes and smiled. "Maybe another time, then."

She reached for the screen door, but before it was half open, Mr. Fine bounded up the steps and ushered her gently across the threshold. The door slammed shut behind them with a bang.

6

WITHIN MINUTES OF SETTING FOOT IN STEELE'S GEM Shop, Henry discovered a painful fact. Mr. Lemberger, the bald man who had taken over the job of repairing watches and necklaces in the glass-walled cubicle at the back of the store, was the exact opposite of Grandpa Jay. The new man not only had no sense of humor, but he also seemed allergic to conversation. Especially with kids.

Henry knew there was something different about Mr. Lemberger the moment he first saw him hunched over his repair tools, as if he was afraid someone might steal them. When Henry approached him to see what he was doing, Mr. Lemberger started coughing as though he had a dinner roll stuck in his throat. He didn't stop until Henry backed off.

The same thing happened when a woman came into the store with her daughter. As soon as the little girl wandered near the glass cubicle, Mr. Lemberger started his awful hacking.

"Mama!" cried the startled child as she ran back to her mother.

Henry was convinced that having Mr. Lemberger working in Grandpa Jay's place had to be bad for business. With him around, the jewelry store was worse than boring. It felt like jail.

Henry paced across the floor like a caged bear, up and back, back and forth, up and back, back and forth, straying close to Mr. Lemberger every now and then to hear him hack, just to break the monotony.

"What's wrong, Henry?" asked Grandma Martha.

"Nothing."

"Henry?"

"What?"

"Would you like to go explore Main Street?"

Henry couldn't hold back his surprise. "By myself?"

"Yes." Grandma Martha held out a dollar bill. "In case you want to get a treat."

"Thanks!"

Henry hurried out the door with his backpack.

Downtown Greenville, of course, was no more exciting than the jewelry store. All the shops looked as sleepy as Tobias Sweet dozing on a bench in front of the bank. Two teenagers slouched in front of the Piggly Wiggly, smoking cigarettes. Henry recognized the lanky one wearing a white apron. He was the guy Henry had almost tripped over on the steps of the church. His stocky, bucktoothed friend wore a gray shirt with the words NELSON'S HARDWARE stitched over the front pocket.

Henry nodded to them as he passed. The lanky one ignored him. His friend blew smoke out of his nose and stared at Henry, bug-eyed. Henry knew it wasn't worth smiling.

Kitty-corner from the supermarket stood the library. The building was closed for repairs, but its front lawn looked a lot more inviting than the front of the Piggly Wiggly. Henry crossed the street, sat down on the grass, and unzipped his backpack, dumping his beanbags and the new juggling book onto the ground.

"The cascade is the simplest of all juggling moves," he read on the first page. "Start with one bag, throwing it up and down in your hand. Then toss it from hand to hand in a figure-eight pattern."

A picture showed a boy demonstrating the move. It seemed simple enough. Henry got to his feet. He tossed one of the bags up and down a few times, then tried the figure-eight pattern. As soon as he stopped, he heard someone clap.

Henry looked across the street. The two teenagers were watching him. He turned away.

"Once you have mastered the figure eight, you are ready for step two," the book continued. "Take three beanbags. While holding a bag in the palm of each hand, throw the third back and forth with your fingertips."

Henry forgot about the two teenagers as he worked to keep his tosses smooth and even. He was getting good.

Now ready for step three, Henry held two bags in his right hand, the third in his left. The object was to throw one bag from his right hand and, while that bag was still in midair, to follow it with a toss from his left hand. The two beanbags had to cross in flight and wind up in the opposite hand.

Henry dropped eleven bags before he made his first successful cross. Once he mastered that move, he tried throwing the bags at different speeds. He was beginning to work up a sweat.

"Yoo-hoo! Henry!" Grandma Martha waved to him from the jewelry shop's doorway. "Time for lunch."

"But, Grandma," he complained, then stopped, knowing too well that he would have plenty of time to practice his juggling in the days ahead. As he crossed the street he heard laughter.

"Yoo-hoo! Henry!" a voice teased.

He knew who it was without even looking.

There was a letter waiting in the mailbox when they got back to the house. The envelope had "Mr. Henry Stone" written on it in his mother's graceful handwriting. Henry waited until he was in his bedroom to open it. The letter was dated June 15, two days before he had left for Indiana.

Dear Henry,

I didn't want you to wait too long for a letter from home, so I'm writing this to you from work before you leave. I hope you're settled in and having fun by the time you read this.

Staying with Grandma Martha should be very good for both of you. You'll have some peace and quiet, and your grandmother will have some wonderful company. She's been so lonely the past six months since Grandpa Jay died.

My creative-writing teacher had us write a haiku for class. I remember the one you wrote in third grade about water bugs. Here's mine.

*As the sun shines down
the mockingbirds sing about
how I adore you.*

*Love,
Mom*

Henry read the letter over three times in search of an answer to the question he had asked his dad about a divorce, but all he found was information he already knew. His mother was going to summer school to finish her college degree so that she could apply to law school in the spring. When she wasn't in college or doing homework, she worked as a secretary in a law firm. She was very busy.

Are my parents going to get separate houses? Where will I live if they do? Will I have to change homes every week? What about school? When will I get to play with Ben?

Henry crumpled the note into a ball and dropped it into his backpack with his mother's poem about gray violets. There was no reason to write her back now. All he had were questions she wouldn't answer.

7

GRANDMA MARTHA WAS PLANNING TO LEAVE THE Gem Shop at three o'clock so that she and Henry could go for a swim at the public pool, but Phoebe Siskin and Martin Sparks came in at two thirty to look for an engagement ring.

"I want a ruby," said Phoebe, who wore black jeans, a black shirt, and had long straight black hair.

"Rubies are lovely," agreed Grandma Martha.

"But engagement rings are supposed to have diamonds," insisted Martin, whose beige mechanic's uniform and blond hair made him look like a spaceman.

"Diamonds are boring," said Phoebe.

"Mrs. Steele, don't engagement rings always have diamonds?" asked Martin.

"Not always," said Grandma Martha, "but diamonds *are* traditional."

"I want something traditional," declared Martin.

"I don't," said Phoebe.

"How can you not like diamonds?" asked Martin.

"I didn't say I don't like diamonds."

"Then what did you say?"

"I said I wanted a ruby."

"But why?"

"Because I like rubies!"

In another minute they were arguing loudly, and Henry automatically started to hum. He was so distracted that he didn't notice Mr. Lemberger had left his cubicle until the older man started hacking like he had pneumonia right behind him. Phoebe and Martin settled down quickly. Henry relaxed and stopped humming.

"Sorry, Mrs. Steele," said Martin.

"We're nervous about this wedding stuff," Phoebe explained.

"I understand," said Grandma Martha. "We all handle stressful times in different ways."

Henry wondered how much Phoebe and Martin argued. *How long do people who love each other have to argue before they fall out of love? How much have*

*my parents argued since I came to stay in Indiana?
Why can't Mom and Dad have a Mr. Lemberger
around at home to keep things quiet?*

It took Martin and Phoebe over an hour to decide
on a ring, which Henry finally found in one of
Grandma Martha's jewelry catalogs. The ring had a
ladybug-size diamond set in the middle of two baby
ladybug-size rubies.

"Henry, you're our savior," said Phoebe, kissing
him on the cheek. Henry felt his face flush, imagining
it looked like a giant ruby.

Then Tobias Sweet came in.

"My Ethel's going to be eighty next week," he
announced.

"That's grand," said Grandma Martha. "Do you
want to buy something for her birthday?"

"Or is it eighty-five?" wondered Mr. Sweet.
"Hmm . . ."

"Do you want me to phone her to find out?"

"No. It will spoil the surprise. Now, let me
think. . . . We were married in 1945, when she was
twenty-five."

"That would make her eighty-one," said Henry.

Seeing his grandmother quickly wipe her eyes,
Henry wondered if she was thinking about the apple
pies Grandpa Jay had always baked for her birthday,
because he said she was the apple of his eye.

"Or was she twenty-four at the time?"

It took Tobias Sweet forever to remember his wife's true age, eighty-two, and then to select a silver brooch shaped like a dove. By the time he left the shop, it was nearly six o'clock. Grandma Martha didn't even bother to dust the display cases like she usually did at day's end.

"Leroy, would you please close up for me?" she asked Mr. Lemberger. "I'm all worn out."

Mr. Lemberger nodded. "No problem."

Grandma Martha turned to Henry. "I'm sorry, sweetheart," she said, sounding more sad than tired. "I can't make it to the pool."

"That's okay," Henry lied.

They went straight home, and Grandma Martha sat quietly in her rocking chair.

"I can make dinner," Henry offered as she rocked slowly back and forth, her eyes seeming to stare at something far away.

"Thank you, dear, but I can manage," she said. "Why don't you go play in the backyard?"

"I help cook at home all the time."

"Is that so?"

"Yes."

"All right. When I'm ready to start cooking, I'll call you."

Henry felt a wave of homesickness crash upon him as his grandmother leaned back in her chair and closed her eyes. Cooking dinner at home with his parents was one of his favorite activities, when they had the time, that is. His mom's specialty was spaghetti and marinara sauce. She would let Henry break the pasta in half and drop it carefully into the pot of boiling water. Slicing the onions for the sauce, they would feel their eyes burn and make believe they were crying. Then they would laugh. His dad specialized in barbecued chicken. There wasn't much to do besides put the chicken parts in a broiling pan and pour the sauce from the bottle. But they always had fun with the sauce, spreading it all over the chicken with their hands like they were finger painting.

Henry scooped up his backpack and headed outside. In the backyard he dumped his beanbags on the ground and opened his juggling book.

"You are now ready for the fourth and final step of the cascade," he read. "With an underhand motion, toss your first bag. As soon as it peaks, throw again from your other hand. Toss back and forth, keeping your eyes on the bags, not on your hands. Count out loud with each throw. Remember to follow the figure-eight pattern."

Henry tossed the first bag.

"One," he counted. "Two . . ."

He was about to throw the third bag when he dropped bag number two.

He started again. "One . . . two . . . three—" Bag number three fell from his fingers before he could grab it.

"One . . . two . . ." Drop.

"One . . . two . . . three—" Drop.

Henry stretched his shoulders and jiggled his arms to shake away the tightness. Then he took a deep breath, blew it out, and began again.

"One." Drop. "One . . . two—" Drop. Drop. "One . . . two . . . three—" Drop. "One . . . two . . . three—" Drop.

As if taking the beat off of his counting, strains of violin music suddenly cut through the air from the Fines' place.

"One . . . two—" Drop. "One . . . two . . . three—" Drop.

Try as he might, Henry could no longer focus on his tosses. The unfamiliar melody, sad and sweet at the same time, kept breaking his concentration.

Letting his beanbags drop, Henry walked over to the fence and looked for the source of the music. At the far end of the Fines' lawn, away from the house, he glimpsed a cabin, mostly hidden by fir trees. It was smaller than a one-car garage and made of what appeared to be logs. Above its door hung a sign that read IZZY'S PLACE. The music was coming from inside.

Henry leaned against the fence, listening to the violin's soothing song. He closed his eyes and felt as though the music were carrying him up into a tall tree. Perched among a flock of blue jays was his grandfather, waving. In his thoughts Henry could see himself just reaching Grandpa Jay's branch when the violin fell silent, dropping Henry back to the ground, alone.

"Hello, Henry," a voice behind him said, startling him for a moment.

Henry opened his eyes and turned to find Mrs. Fine leaning against her screen door.

"Hello," said Henry.

"Beautiful, wasn't it?"

"Yes."

"That's the way my husband cries."

Henry wasn't sure he understood what she meant, but before he could ask her to explain, the door of the cabin opened and Mr. Fine filled the threshold.

"Do you need anything, Louise?" he asked.

"No, dear. But I'll bet Henry would like a tour of Izzy's Place."

Mr. Fine cleared his throat. "Some other day," he said, lumbering toward the house. "It's time for dinner."

Nodding at Henry, he wished him a "Good evening," then bounded up the back steps to gently usher his wife inside.

Henry gazed at Izzy's Place, certain he could easily sneak over to investigate it by himself. But he knew he wouldn't. Stealing into a little cabin where an old man went to cry would be wrong. He had to have an invitation.

8

THE NEXT MORNING ON THE WAY TO WORK GRANDMA Martha offered to buy Henry some new comic books. He accepted gratefully, but when she stopped the car in front of the Piggly Wiggly, he changed his mind.

"Thanks," he said, "but, actually, I don't need any more comics."

"Then buy yourself a book."

"I don't feel like reading."

"Suit yourself," his grandmother said impatiently.

In fact, he was sick of his old Spiderman comics. But he didn't want to go into the store where he was sure to run into the lanky teenager.

Steele's Gem Shop was even quieter than usual, and Henry couldn't stay still.

"You're going to wear out my floor with all of that pacing," said his grandmother.

"What do you want me to do?" asked Henry.

"Go outside."

"I don't feel like it."

"Then what do you want to do?"

"I don't know."

When Henry stopped to watch Mr. Lemberger fix the broken clasp of a bracelet, Mr. Lemberger spoke to him for the first time.

"What can I do for you, boy?" he asked.

"Nothing," said Henry. "I was just looking at those pearls."

"They're not pearls, they're opals."

"Pearls, opals. Who cares?"

"The customers."

"Big deal."

Henry wondered how his grandmother could have replaced Grandpa Jay with such a boring robot. It made him want to grab the bracelet and throw it out the door.

When Mr. Lemberger replied with a loud cough, Henry seized his backpack and fled outside. For lack of anything else better to do, he began practicing a cascade. On his first try he tossed four bags in a row before dropping one. On his next toss he made it to five. The second the bag hit the ground, someone applauded.

"Yoo-hoo!" a voice teased.

Not again! Out of the corner of his eye he spied two familiar figures in front of the Piggly Wiggly. Henry checked his watch. Ten thirty. *Tomorrow, I'll come out after they take their morning breaks,* he promised himself.

He picked up the dropped bag and started over.

"One . . . two . . . three," he counted aloud. One of the boys whistled. "Four . . . five . . ."

Henry dropped the sixth toss. The boys laughed like jackals. "Jerks," he muttered under his breath.

"Yoo-hoo!" they yelled. "Yoo-hoo!"

Henry struggled to ignore them.

"One . . . two . . . three . . . four—" Drop, drop.

The boys laughed louder. Unable to contain himself any longer, Henry imitated them, pitching his voice an octave higher and laughing over and over to exaggerate how stupid they sounded. His fake laugh echoed through the air unanswered. The boys across the street were silent.

Henry picked up his dropped beanbags and resumed juggling.

"One . . . two . . . three . . . four . . ."

The silence continued.

Henry thought someone might be approaching, but he refused to look around.

"Five . . . six . . . seven . . ."

He could hear both teenagers getting closer, and still he held his ground.

"Eight . . . nine . . ."

Suddenly, a hand swooped in and grabbed one of his bags.

"Ten!" shouted the bucktoothed boy.

"Give me that!" cried Henry.

The teenagers laughed as they threw the stolen beanbag back and forth across the lawn.

"Yoo-hoo!"

"Yoo-hoo!"

Henry ran after them desperately, but the older boys were faster and more agile. They ran past and around him, keeping the beanbag well beyond his reach. When the lanky boy elbowed him aside, knocking him to the ground, Henry lost all fear. He was not a fighter, but his anger spurred him on. Throwing his arms around the boy's waist, he held on tightly.

"Let go, or you're going to be sorry," warned the boy.

"Give me my beanbag!" demanded Henry.

"Let go!"

"Give me my beanbag!!"

Henry felt a searing pain as the other boy yanked his hair. He stumbled backward and fell. In another moment they had him pinned to the ground, with a boy kneeling on each of his arms.

"Think you're tough, twerp?" jeered the buck-toothed boy.

"Give me my beanbag," Henry said with clenched teeth.

"Answer the question," ordered the lanky boy.

Their bony knees pressing upon his arms pinched his skin.

"You get your kicks picking on littler kids?" Henry tried not to cry.

"You came after me," answered the lanky boy.

"You stole my beanbag!"

"You stole my beanbag," mimicked the boy.

"You stole my beanbag," repeated his friend.

"Excuse me!" a deep voice broke in.

Before either teenager could say another word, someone grabbed them by the backs of their shirts and hoisted them to their feet. They struggled against Mr. Fine's huge fists, but he held them firm.

"I was driving past and wondered what you fellows were up to," he said, his voice calm and quiet.

"We were just kiddin' around," said the buck-toothed boy, dropping Henry's beanbag.

"It didn't look like kidding around to me, William," said Mr. Fine.

He shook the boys again.

"William, I know it's been a while since I had you in eighth-grade science, so you've probably forgotten what I think of bullies."

"No, Mr. Fine," William said weakly. "I remember."

"It's been even longer since I taught you, Raymond, so I'm *sure* you've forgotten."

The lanky boy shook his head. "I remember too."

"You both just had momentary memory lapses, right?"

They nodded.

"I understand."

He released them, their faces red with anger.

"We all need a refresher course now and again." Mr. Fine picked up his fallen baseball cap and slapped it against his knee to clean off the dirt. "I'll bet you probably forgot what you learned with me about soil types, too."

Looking at Henry for the first time, he asked, "Are you hurt, son?"

"No," Henry said, getting to his feet.

"Good." Mr. Fine stared at the teenagers. "Now would you gentlemen please pick up those beanbags and give them back to my friend here."

Raymond and William did as Mr. Fine asked without another word, then hurried back to the Piggly Wiggly.

Henry turned to Mr. Fine.

"Thanks," he said reluctantly.

"You're welcome," said Mr. Fine. "Does your grandmother know where you are?"

"Yes."

"All right, then."

Henry had a lot more to say, but Mr. Fine quickly turned and tromped back to his green van before Henry could get the words out.

"Hey!" Henry managed to shout as the van started up.

Mr. Fine didn't hear, of course. His windows were closed, and the engine was too loud. Fuming, Henry watched the van disappear down Main Street, then stuffed his beanbags into his backpack and kicked the pack all the way to the jewelry store.

9

As soon as he got home, Henry marched over to the Fines' house. He rang the front doorbell and waited for a while, but there was no answer. He rang a second time and waited even longer, standing on the porch like a polite trick-or-treater. After a third ring he gave up.

Halfway back to Grandma Martha's house, he heard Mrs. Fine calling him.

"Did you want something, Henry?"

Henry turned back. Dressed in a bathrobe, Mrs. Fine stood in her doorway with one frail hand propped against the doorpost, her eyelids heavy with sleep, as if she had just woken up from a nap.

"Sorry to bother you," said Henry.

"You weren't bothering me, dear. I was just slow getting to the door." She shivered as if trying to shake off sleep and gave him an encouraging smile. "What can I do for you?"

"I need to tell Mr. Fine something."

Mrs. Fine nodded toward the back of the house. "Ernie said he was going to weed in the garden, but I suspect he's in his hideout by now."

"Izzy's Place?"

"Yes. Izzy's Place." Mrs. Fine sighed. "Try him there."

"Okay," said Henry.

He watched her hobble back inside the house, like her feet were weighed down with cement, then headed off to find Mr. Fine.

Mrs. Fine was right; the yard was empty. Then Henry heard violin music coming from the cabin. As soon as he knocked, the music stopped and the door opened.

Mr. Fine gazed down at Henry. "What can I do for you?"

Henry looked up at him and boldly said, "I didn't need your help before with those two boys."

"Is that so?"

"Yes."

"Why is that?"

"I can take care of myself."

"How old are you?"

"Ten and a half."

"I see." Mr. Fine scratched his chin and stared at Henry uncertainly. "Was there anything else you wanted to tell me?"

"No."

"All right, then. Next time I see anyone beating you up, I'll look the other way."

"They weren't beating me up."

"What were they doing?"

"They were teasing me."

"It looked like pretty rough teasing to me."

"It wasn't."

Grandma Martha interrupted their conversation, calling from her back door. "Henry, your daddy's on the phone."

"I'm talking to Mr. Fine."

"You can speak with him after you finish talking to your daddy."

"This is important."

"Henry, I'm not asking you to come," Grandma Martha said sharply. "I'm telling you!"

Before Henry could object, Mr. Fine tapped him on the shoulder. "I'll be here," he said. "Better not keep your old man waiting."

His dad had his chipper voice on when Henry picked up the phone.

"Hi, champ," he said. "How're you doing?"

"Okay," said Henry.

"What's new?

"Nothing."

"Grandma says you've made friends with her neighbor."

"We're not really friends."

"Are there any kids your age on the block?"

"I don't know." Henry lowered his voice. "Grandma won't even let me leave the house by myself."

"I'll talk to her."

"It won't help."

"Yes, it will."

"Whatever."

They were both quiet for a while.

"I miss you, pal," said his dad.

In the silence Henry tried to will himself back home, sitting in the kitchen together with his dad and mom, but the thought remained only a picture in his mind. Henry felt his throat tighten and knew that if he didn't get off the phone soon, he would start crying.

"You want to talk to Grandma?" he asked.

"Yes," said his father. "Take care of yourself, kiddo."

"Bye."

Henry brushed back tears and handed the receiver

to Grandma Martha. He wandered out of the kitchen and found Mr. Fine standing in the middle of his yard, holding something bright red in his hand.

"Catch," said Mr. Fine.

Mr. Fine threw the thing high into the air, but Henry didn't feel like running after it. He had used up too much energy trying to be strong on the phone with his dad. As the red object dropped toward him two wings opened from its sides. Gliding gently over the fence into Grandma Martha's yard, it sang, *what-chew, what-chew,* as it landed at Henry's feet.

It was a model cardinal, so lifelike that Henry first thought it was real. Everything about it, from its scarlet backswept crest and black face to its long, tapered tail, seemed perfect. Henry could imagine the bird cracking open a seed with its bill to get at the kernel inside.

"Found it years ago in a hobby shop in Indianapolis," said Mr. Fine. "What do you think?"

Henry shrugged. "It's okay." Just picking up the toy bird took his remaining bit of energy.

The Fines' kitchen door squealed open, and Mrs. Fine appeared on the threshold wearing a yellow dress. Her husband looked at her with interest.

"Dinner should be ready in ten minutes," she said.

"Be right in," said Mr. Fine.

Mr. Fine watched his wife go back inside, a smile

brightening his face. "First time she's made dinner in weeks," he said.

"Here." Henry tossed the bird back across the fence.

Mr. Fine caught it and stroked its head. "You want to keep it for the night?"

"Nah."

"You sure?"

Henry nodded, blinking away tears.

"You look like you could use something to cheer you up."

"No, I don't. I'm fine."

"No, I'm Fine. You're Stone."

Henry didn't smile.

"Well," said Mr. Fine. "I hope you feel better in the morning." Then he tucked the bird under his arm and followed his wife into the house.

During dinner Henry pushed the peas and carrots back and forth across his plate without eating any of them. He didn't even touch his meat loaf.

Grandma Martha broke the silence first. "Mrs. Mollenhoffer has a grandson who's just your age," she said. "His name is Carl."

Henry didn't respond.

"I thought I'd call her to arrange a play date for you."

Henry remained silent.

"Don't you want to have a playmate your own age?"

Henry crushed a pea with his fork.

"Henry?"

"I don't care." He didn't even care enough to tell her that *playmate* was a kindergarten word.

"I think you do."

"Well, I think you're wrong!"

"Don't yell at me!"

"I wasn't yelling."

"It sounded like yelling to me."

Henry crushed another pea with his fork.

"Henry."

"What?"

"Please stop doing that and look at me."

Henry put down his fork. "What?" he said, keeping his eyes on the table.

"I know you're sad about your parents. And I know that if Grandpa Jay were here, he could do a better job of keeping your mind off of them than I can. But he's not . . ."

Grandma Martha fell silent. When Henry looked up, he found her staring at the ceiling as if she were searching for heaven.

"When Grandpa Jay died," she continued in a low voice, "I lost the only man I ever loved. But I didn't give up on life." His grandmother reached out to brush a strand of hair from Henry's forehead. "You shouldn't either."

Grandma Martha finished the rest of her dinner without another word. Leaving his food uneaten, Henry excused himself from the table and went to his room. Before bed he tossed twenty beanbags in a row without a miss.

10

WHEN HE CAME DOWN FOR BREAKFAST THE NEXT morning, Henry found Grandma Martha humming in the kitchen.

"I spoke to Mrs. Mollenhoffer last night after you went to bed," she told him. "She said she would talk to Carl and call me back this afternoon."

"Why?" asked Henry, playing dumb.

"Why what?"

Grandma Martha set two plates of scrambled eggs and bacon with toast on the table and sat down across from Henry.

"Why does she need to talk to Carl today?" Henry persisted.

"We went over that last night." Grandma Martha speared a forkful of egg.

"Went over what?"

Grandma Martha chewed and swallowed her food before she said, "Henry, I don't like this game you're playing."

"What game?"

"You know what game."

"No, I don't."

"Do you want a playmate or not?"

"*Playmate* is a kindergarten word."

"Well, that's very appropriate, since you're acting like a grumpy kindergartner."

"So what?"

Henry saw the loose skin around his grandmother's jaw tighten, but instead of saying anything, she cut a piece of bacon in half and ate one of the pieces, then followed that with a bite of toast. She began humming again as she cleared the table and washed the dishes and was still humming as they got into the station wagon. She hummed as she put the key in the ignition and turned it. The engine answered her with a *spit, spit spit, cough, cough,* then clanked to a stop.

Grandma Martha turned the key again, but this time the engine spit just once and died. *Serves her right for acting so cheerful,* Henry thought.

The heavy hood, with its rusted hinges, was hard to open. His grandmother needed his help to lift it.

"Do you know anything about cars?" she asked him.

"Nope," replied Henry. "I'm only good with crayons."

"Now, don't be smart with me."

"Don't *you* be smart with me."

"Henry, that's enough! I've done nothing to deserve such treatment. I can't help it if Grandpa Jay's not here to amuse you and if your parents—" Grandma Martha stopped.

"If my parents what?" demanded Henry.

"Nothing."

"If my parents what?" insisted Henry.

"I'm sorry if your parents have made you so angry," said Grandma Martha finally.

"That's not what you were going to say."

"You're right. I was going to say I'm sorry that your parents are having problems, but there's nothing you or I can do about it. The only thing we can do something about is our own anger."

She brushed a speck of rust off of her sleeve, then went inside to call for help. Henry took his beanbags out of his backpack. He threw one of them high in the air and let it hit the sidewalk. He hurled the second bag up even higher and kicked it as it came down. The bag went flying into a rosebush.

"Nice shot," a familiar bass voice said behind him.

Henry didn't reply.

"Is something wrong with your grandmother's car?"

"Who knows?"

"If anyone does, you should."

Henry spun around to argue, but he couldn't get any words out when he saw Mr. Fine lumbering toward him. He was wearing a bright orange bathrobe with brown tiger stripes.

"What are you gawking at?" asked Mr. Fine.

"What do you think?" Henry replied, eyeing the robe.

"It was a gift, so watch what you say."

Henry smirked. "Yes, sir."

Mr. Fine walked up to the car and peered under the hood. Henry retrieved his beanbag from the rosebush and began to juggle, counting the throws to himself. *One, two, three, four, five . . .* The cascade was almost easy now.

"Henry, go tell your grandma to call off the tow truck," said Mr. Fine. "I think I can help her."

Mr. Fine reached into the engine and yanked out a black band of rubber split through the middle.

"Busted fan belt." He dropped it on the sidewalk like a dead snake. "Be right back."

Grandma Martha sat at the kitchen table, idly doodling on a notepad as she cradled the phone receiver against her ear.

"It's been busy this whole time," she told Henry. "That lovesick Martin Sparks must be gabbing away with his fiancée."

"Mr. Fine says he can fix it."

"What?" Hanging up the phone, Grandma Martha scurried outside. Henry paused to study the doodling on her notepad. From a distance it appeared to be a plain oblong shape. But upon closer examination he saw that she had drawn a pipe just like the one Grandpa Jay used to smoke. Henry could almost smell the cherry tobacco his grandfather liked best.

The picture of the pipe reminded Henry how different things were now. Just a year ago Grandpa Jay would have fixed the car himself, one, two, three. And he would have made a game of it, wrestling the broken fan belt to the ground as if it were alive or maybe pulling a screwdriver out of Henry's nose. Grandma Martha had probably been thinking the same thing while she was on the phone.

Henry ripped the sketch out of the notepad and stuffed it into his pocket, then wandered outside, where he found Mr. Fine, now dressed in overalls, fiddling with the engine, a pair of brown suspenders slung over one of his shoulders. His huge hands worked skillfully as he cut a large section from the suspenders and fit it on to two grooved wheels connected to the engine.

"When the crankshaft moves, it should turn the suspenders, which should turn the fan to keep the engine cool," he explained. "A fairly simple solution, assuming it works."

"I'm sure it will," Grandma Martha said. "I have confidence in you, Ernie."

Mr. Fine turned toward Henry, sitting abjectly on his grandmother's porch steps. "How about you, Henry?"

"What?"

"Do you think the car will run?"

"I don't care."

"Henry," warned his grandmother, "that's not the proper way to talk."

"That's all right, Martha," Mr. Fine intervened. "Let's see what happens."

Grandma Martha slid behind the steering wheel and turned the key. *Cough, clank, spit, spit, spit, whirrrrr . . .*

"You're a magician," she said.

Mr. Fine shook his head. "Tell me that *after* you've made it to the gas station."

Grandma Martha wanted to pay Mr. Fine for his work, but he wouldn't let her. "I don't charge for suspender installations," he said. "But I'd like to give Henry something."

Reaching into a pocket of his overalls, Mr. Fine pulled out a thick rubber worm with a zipper along its belly. "If you unzip it, you'll find something interesting inside," he said, offering it to Henry.

"That's okay."

"You sure?" Mr. Fine extended the worm toward him.

Henry shook his head and got into the backseat. Grandma Martha frowned.

"Oh, all right," he said, giving in.

Grandma Martha thanked Mr. Fine again and waved to him as they drove off. She said nothing to Henry.

11

THE WORM LAY ON THE BACKSEAT SHAPED LIKE A question mark beside Henry.

"Why did you do that?" asked Grandma Martha.

"Do what?"

"Act so rude."

"I wasn't rude."

"You most certainly were."

"I didn't want him to give me a present."

"Why on earth not?"

"I wasn't in the mood."

"He was trying to make you feel better."

"I don't care."

"Yes, you do."

"No, I don't."

"If you didn't care, you wouldn't be so angry."

"Who said I'm angry?"

"I think it's perfectly obvious."

"You think you know everything."

"No, I don't. But I do know something about being angry. Last winter after I lost Grandpa Jay, I was angry a lot. And sad, too. And usually both at the same time."

"You had a good reason."

"So do you. And so does Ernie Fine. It's how we live with our anger and sadness that counts."

They drove on without another word, which was fine with Henry. He didn't feel like being told he was rude and angry and sad. All he wanted was to go home and turn back the clock to a happier time, like the spring night when his dad came home from work with a bunch of daffodils for his mom and a choco-late cigar for him, and they ate dinner at Maria's Pizzeria and afterward went bowling at Carolier Lanes. Henry was in second grade then, and his dad and Mr. Kahn had just become partners, and the rug store was new and promised to make them lots of money. And his parents almost never argued.

The car engine clicked like a stuttering metronome as Grandma Martha pulled into Martin Sparks's gas station. When Martin lifted the hood and saw Mr.

Fine's suspender installation, he whistled.

"What the hey?"

Grandma Martha explained the situation, and Martin whistled again. "That's ingenuity for you," he said respectfully.

Martin promised the car would be ready by lunch. He offered to give them a ride to the jewelry store, but Grandma Martha said they could walk the four blocks. As she and Henry were about to leave she gave Henry a look.

"What?" he asked.

"Don't you want to know what's inside?"

"Inside what?"

She reached through the car's back window and pulled out the worm. "Your gift."

"I don't care."

Grandma Martha sighed and unzipped it herself. Inside the worm she found a piece of paper with a message that she read out loud.

"Question: 'What did the earthworm say to the glowworm when they met at the barn dance?'

"Answer: 'Ah, light of my life, I have finally found you.'"

Henry didn't think the punch line was very funny, but it made Grandma Martha giggle. Martin laughed too.

"I'll have to tell that one to Phoebe," he said.

12

THAT AFTERNOON ANOTHER LETTER WAS WAITING for Henry when he and Grandma Martha got home from the jewelry store. Henry took the steps two at a time as he hurried to his room to read it.

Dear Henry,

College classes and work have been keeping me very busy. I asked my boss for a raise yesterday, and he agreed. Now I can really start saving money for law school.

I hope you'll write to me soon to let me know how you and Grandma Martha are doing. And I'll try to phone you so I can hear your voice.

   *Meanwhile, my creative-writing teacher had us
each write a sonnet. I wrote mine for you. Here it is.*

   *I wish I knew the best way to explain
   Why Dad and I have grown so far apart,
   And why we fight and cause each other pain
   When once upon a time we shared one heart.
   I wish that I could fix things with this poem
   So that we three would fall back into place
   And life would be like it was in our home
   When smiles were more familiar to your face.
   But though we know some wishes don't come true,
   That life works out in many different ways,
   Please know that whenever it comes to you,
   Your dad and I will love you all our days.
   No matter what, you'll always be our boy
   For whom we wish a life of peace and joy.*

                              *Love,
                               Mom*

   Henry couldn't tell if the poem really meant his parents were going to get a divorce or not. All it said was "no matter what," and that wasn't explanation enough.

   He tried to write back but could only manage, "Dear Mom, I hate your poem," before he crumpled up the fancy notepaper she had given him and threw it away. What was the point of writing if there was nothing he could do to change things? After stuffing his mother's letter into his backpack, he trudged downstairs.

Grandma Martha had baked Mr. Fine a raspberry pie and asked Henry to deliver it. The pie tin was still warm as he carried it across the alley. There was no answer at the Fines' front door, so Henry went around back, where he found Mrs. Fine lying on a lawn chair. He couldn't see her eyes beneath her sunglasses, but her stillness told him she was asleep. She looked exhausted as she lay there, her breathing shallow, her skin the color of the sky on a cloudy winter day.

Henry left her alone and walked back to the cabin. He was about to knock when the door opened and Mr. Fine filled the entrance.

"Hello, Henry," he said.

"This is from my grandmother." Henry handed him the pie. "For the suspender installation."

"Very kind of her. What flavor is it?"

"Raspberry."

Mr. Fine gazed across the yard at his sleeping wife, then looked back at Henry. "Do you like raspberry pie?"

"I guess so."

"Why do you have to guess? Don't you know?"

"I like it okay."

"Do you want a piece?"

Henry shrugged.

"Was that shoulder twitch a yes or a no?"

"A yes, I guess."

Mr. Fine stepped back inside the cabin, leaving the door open behind him. Henry hesitated on the threshold and looked up at the sign that read IZZY'S PLACE, wondering why Mr. Fine had suddenly decided to invite him in.

"Are you coming or not?" called Mr. Fine.

Henry shrugged again and entered.

A violin case rested on a wooden folding chair in the middle of the room, which looked like a small laboratory. Against one wall stood a slate-topped worktable covered with test tubes, beakers, and graduated cylinders. Measuring spoons, tweezers, forceps, and scalpels hung on the wall above the worktable, and on a separate table there lay a microscope, a Bunsen burner, a voltage meter, a pair of scales, and other pieces of equipment Henry had never even seen before. And there was more.

Jars of all shapes and sizes containing different-colored chemicals took up two entire shelves on one wall. Below the shelves towered a tall bookcase stacked with hundreds of finger-thin glass bottles, all filled with what looked like brown and black dirt and marked with square, white labels. That so much stuff could fit into such a small room was quite amazing. Even more amazing to Henry was how neat the room was. Nothing looked out of place.

Tucked in one corner of the room was a small sink, where Mr. Fine was washing his hands like a surgeon about to operate. Once finished, he waited for Henry to do the same. He then picked up the violin case, placed it on top of the bookcase, and set the pie tin on the folding chair.

"After you," he said.

"After me, what?" asked Henry.

"After you sit, then I will."

"Where should I sit?"

"On your bottom," said Mr. Fine with a straight face. "Watch, I'll demonstrate."

He carefully folded his massive legs beneath himself like a jumbo jet pulling up its landing gear and settled down on the floor in a half lotus position, impressing Henry with his flexibility.

"Now you try it."

Henry quickly sat beside him.

"I assume you know how to eat pie with your fingers," said Mr. Fine.

"Why?"

"Because I have no forks."

"With all the stuff in this cabin you don't have a fork?"

"That's correct." Mr. Fine sounded serious. "Anyway, they say a good piece of pie is best appreciated with one's fingers."

"Who's 'they'?" asked Henry, unconvinced.

"Good question."

Mr. Fine scooped two of his massive fingers into the pie, broke off a large piece, and popped it into his mouth. He sighed as he chewed.

"Help yourself," he said, handing Henry the pie tin.

"Thanks."

Henry spooned out a chunk of pie with his pointer finger and ate it slowly.

"What do you think?" asked Mr. Fine.

"I think I like blueberry more."

"I didn't ask what you like more, I asked what you thought of this particular pie."

"It's okay."

"Just okay?" Mr. Fine wiped a dab of burgundy-colored filling from his cheek. "Humph."

"I like the pie," Henry replied. "But whatever *they* say, I think *I* could appreciate it better with a fork."

Mr. Fine stared at Henry, a look of surprise on his face. His shoulders started to shake and a sound bubbled up from his chest, spread to his throat, and spilled out of his mouth as a whinny. Soon, in spite of himself, Henry was laughing too.

In the distance they could hear Grandma Martha calling. "Yoo-hoo, Henry! You've got company."

∽ 13 ∾

HENRY FOUND HIS COMPANY IN THE KITCHEN TALKING to Grandma Martha. Or, rather, she talked while he chewed gum.

"Carl Mollenhoffer," she said, "Henry Stone."

A bucktoothed boy about Henry's age, Carl blew a pink bubble and popped it. Henry thought he looked oddly familiar.

"I didn't know we were having a guest," Henry said.

"I wanted it to be a surprise," replied his grand-mother.

"I don't like surprises."

"That's a pity. Now go out and play. I'll call you for dinner."

Grandma Martha gave Henry a do-what-I-say-or-else stare as she ushered him and Carl out the kitchen door.

Gazing around the yard, Carl blew a fist-size bubble, plucked it out of his mouth, pinched it closed with his dirty fingers, then tossed it up in the air and caught it on the tip of his thumb. Henry wasn't impressed.

"Don't you even have a basketball hoop?" asked Carl.

"Nope," said Henry. "This is it."

Carl popped the bubble and stuffed the wad of gum back into his mouth. He wandered over to Grandpa Jay's tree swing and kicked it. The plank wobbled back and forth like a drunken pendulum.

"Don't do that," Henry told him.

"Do what?" Carl kicked the swing again.

"That." Henry caught the wobbling swing and let it gently hang down to rest.

"My mom said I had to come over here as a favor to my grandmother," said Carl.

"You're a very good grandson," said Henry sarcastically.

"I know." Carl kicked the swing again.

Again, Henry stopped it.

If this is Grandma Martha's idea of company,

Henry thought, *I'll take solitary confinement.*

As the two boys glared at each other Mr. Fine's violin pierced the air like a steam whistle.

"What's that?" asked Carl.

"My neighbor," said Henry.

"Who's your neighbor?"

"Mr. Fine."

"Your neighbor is Mr. Fine?"

"Yes."

"Ernie Fine, the old science teacher?"

"Right."

Carl climbed onto the fence and stared at the cabin. He blew another bubble and popped it.

"Who's Izzy? Ernie the Ape's kid?"

"I don't know. And he's not an ape."

"What's in there?"

"Mr. Fine's laboratory."

"Wait till I tell Willie."

"Who's Willie?"

"My brother."

Henry walked over to the fence to look at Carl more closely. Now Henry knew why Carl looked familiar. He had the same buckteeth as the teenager who took his beanbag.

"Your brother works at the hardware store, doesn't he?"

"Yep. And he hates Mr. Fine. Willie says the old man was picking on him and Ray yesterday."

"No, he wasn't."

Carl jumped off the fence. "How do you know?"

"I was there."

Carl smirked. "*You're* the lousy juggler?"

"I'm *not* a lousy juggler."

"Yes, you are."

"No, I'm not. You've never even seen me juggle."

"I don't have to. I heard all about you, Juggles."

"Don't call me that."

"Why not, Juggles?"

"Shut up."

"Make me, Juggles!" Strutting up to him, Carl blew a bubble in his face and popped it.

Drops of saliva splattered against Henry's cheek. He wiped them off with the back of his hand.

"You disgusting jerk."

"Juggles!"

Henry shoved Carl backward hard; Carl answered with his fists. When Grandma Martha called the boys in for dinner, she found them wrestling on the ground, their shirts bloody.

∽ 14 ∽

"HENRY STONE, I'M ASHAMED OF YOU."

"He started it."

"He said you pushed him."

"He popped a bubble in my face!"

"So you pushed him?"

"Yes."

"Hold still."

"Ouch!"

Grandma Martha poured hydrogen peroxide on Henry's elbow where Carl had bitten him, the outline of his sharp buckteeth perfectly clear. The antiseptic solution bubbled around the wound like ocean foam as

Henry's arm throbbed. He didn't mind, though. His enemy had left with a bloody nose and a welt on his neck. Henry was proud of himself for standing up to Carl. He was a bully just like his bucktoothed brother.

"What am I going to do with you?" said Grandma Martha as she dabbed at Henry's elbow with a cotton ball.

"I don't care."

Grandma Martha dropped the cotton ball in the trash. "Well, I do."

"I don't."

Grandma Martha reached for Henry to pull him toward her, but he held firmly in his place.

"I don't want to be hugged," he said.

"Please," she pleaded.

Henry softened a little, enough to allow her to wrap her arms around him, but he did not return her embrace.

"It's okay to let yourself be mothered," said Grandma Martha. "It doesn't mean you're a baby, just human."

As she gently rubbed first-aid cream over his wound Henry softened more and let his chin rest on her shoulder while she covered his wound with a bandage.

Over dinner they agreed that Carl was not good company.

"He strikes me as a rude child," declared Grandma Martha.

"I think he's a fart-breathing moron," said Henry.

"Henry, please."

"It's true!"

"Even if it is," said Grandma Martha, trying not to laugh, "you don't have to say it out loud."

After the dishes were washed, they watched a game show on television. Grandma Martha relaxed in her rocker while Henry nestled in Grandpa Jay's easy chair, rubbing his cheek against the plush velvet upholstery. They both fell asleep in their chairs and didn't wake up until the late news came on.

The phone rang the next morning during breakfast. Henry reached it first.

"Hey, champ. What's new?"

"I, uh—" Henry looked at his grandmother. "I got into a fight yesterday."

"Not with Grandma Martha, I hope."

"No. Some kid she introduced me to."

"Did you get hurt?"

"A couple of scratches and some teeth marks."

"How about him?"

"A bloody nose."

"Who started it?"

"We both did."

"Sounds like you haven't made a friend yet."

"No kidding."

"How are things otherwise?" His dad sounded like he was reading questions from a checklist.

"I can do a cascade now."

"What's a cascade?"

"It's a basic juggling move."

"Terrific. So life isn't all bad, is it?"

Henry knew it wasn't worth complaining. "Everything's fine," he said. "Just terrific."

"Great. Let me speak to your grandma."

Henry handed her the phone and went to sit on the front porch. He already knew what she had to say about the fight.

People drove by the house on the way to work. Morning rush-hour traffic in Greenville meant a couple of cars and some delivery trucks. There wasn't much to look at except for one beat-up black convertible that stopped by the Fines' house.

The driver and his two passengers stepped out and walked down the alley. Henry recognized Carl, Willie, and Ray at once, but they didn't notice him. They were too busy spying on Izzy's Place.

On their way back to their car Henry heard Willie say, "Tonight."

The three boys slapped high fives, then got into the convertible and sped off.

∼ 15 ∼

Lyn Grackle stopped by the jewelry store moments after Grandma Martha opened the door.

"Today's our anniversary bash," she said. "We're cutting the cake at noon."

"We'll be there," said Grandma Martha.

Lyn gave Henry a nod. "Madge and I are givin' free haircuts today to gals and fellas under twelve."

"I don't need a haircut," said Henry.

"Don't you like buzz cuts?"

"No."

"A little trim wouldn't hurt." Lyn eyed Henry. "We're losin' sight of your ears."

"I like it that way."

"Someone who knows what he wants." Lyn winked at him. "I like that in a man."

She patted Henry on the shoulder, then turned to Mr. Lemberger.

"Leroy, you're welcome for cake too," she said, "even if that bald head of yours hasn't set foot in our shop for years."

Mr. Lemberger set down the watch he was working on and thought for a moment. "Thank you," he said. "I'll try to stop by."

Henry was surprised to see him smile.

"I'll save you a piece with a cow on it," said Lyn. She nodded at Henry. "A lot of my best customers are either farmers or retired ones, like Leroy here." Then she winked at him again and left.

Grandma Martha watched her through the front window. "Lyn loves to flirt with all the men in town," she explained. "But she's a very nice person and an excellent haircutter."

For the rest of that morning Henry kept thinking about Carl, Willie, and Ray. He thought about them when he went to have some anniversary cake at lunchtime and again refused a free buzz cut from Lyn. He couldn't stop thinking about them all afternoon, either.

The word *tonight* in itself was perfectly harmless, but with those three it took on an ominous tone. Henry felt sure they were planning something.

When he got back to the house, Henry headed for Izzy's Place. He knocked on the cabin door, and it opened at once.

"Oh," said Mr. Fine with apparent disappointment. "Hello, Henry."

"Sorry to bother you," said Henry.

"No bother. I thought you might be Louise."

"How is she feeling today?"

"So-so." Mr. Fine sighed. "What can I do for you?"

"I have something important to tell you."

"Come in."

Mr. Fine pointed to the wooden chair beside his worktable. As Henry sat down he noticed that one of the small bottles from the bookcase lay open on the table beside the microscope. Mr. Fine screwed the top back on the jar and shut off the little light on the microscope.

"What's in the bottle?" asked Henry.

"What's it look like?" replied Mr. Fine.

"Dirt."

"That's what it is: dirt." Mr. Fine carried the bottle to the bookcase.

"What do you do with it?"

"I look at it under the microscope."

"Why?"

"I want to see what's in it."

"Are all those bottles filled with dirt?"

"Yes."

"Where did you get it?"

"I've collected samples from every place Louise and I have ever visited."

"Looks like you've visited a lot of places."

"All fifty states. And thirty-seven foreign countries." Mr. Fine carefully set the bottle in its proper place. "Now that I've answered all of your questions, what's the important thing you came to tell me?"

"Some guys were snooping around this cabin this morning."

"What did they look like?"

"You remember the ones who were picking on me?"

"You mean William Mollenhoffer and Raymond Getz."

"Yes. They were here with Willie's brother, Carl. I think they're planning to play a trick on you."

"What makes you think so?"

"I heard them say, 'Tonight.'"

"Well, I'll keep a lookout, then." Mr. Fine studied Henry. "Awful neighborly of you," he said, offering his hand. "Thanks for the warning."

"You're welcome."

Henry understood that the handshake was Mr. Fine's way of saying good-bye, but he had one more question.

"Why do you call this 'Izzy's Place'?"

"Why do you want to know?"

"I was just wondering. I never heard a name like that."

"It's a nickname for 'Isaac.'"

"Is he your son?"

"He was." Mr. Fine looked up at the ceiling. "Izzy died when he was little."

"Sorry," said Henry. "I didn't know."

Mr. Fine shook his head. "There's nothing to apologize about."

Afraid of saying the wrong thing, Henry moved toward the door. "I, uh, have to go now."

Mr. Fine nodded, and Henry hurried away.

∽ 16 ∾

GRANDMA MARTHA WAS SLICING ONIONS AND TALKING on the phone as Henry reached the kitchen. Her eyes were shiny. At first Henry thought it was because of the onions, but when she offered him the phone and said, "It's your mommy," he felt his throat tighten.

"What's wrong?" he asked.

"Who said anything was wrong?"

She set the receiver on the counter and left Henry alone. His throat tightened harder as he picked up the phone.

"Hi, honey." His mom sounded too cheerful. "How's my guy?"

"Okay. Why are you calling?"

"I just got home from work, and I wanted to hear your voice."

"Why was Grandma crying?"

"I didn't know she was crying."

"I saw."

"Now, Henry."

"Are you and Dad getting divorced?"

"Darling, I called to see how you were, not to talk about Dad and me."

"Are you?" Henry persisted.

"We've been talking about it. But we're not doing anything until you come home."

"So that means you are."

"I didn't say that."

"You don't have to. I can tell from the way you're talking and Grandma's crying."

"Honey . . ."

"I have to go."

His eyes blurry with tears, Henry hung up and ran upstairs to his room. Moments after he locked his door and threw himself on his bed, he heard the phone ring.

"Henry," his grandmother called. "Mommy wants to talk to you again."

"We already talked."

Henry reached for his beanbags.

"She has more to say."

"I don't care."

His first throw hit the ceiling.

"Henry."

"One . . . Two . . . Three."

"Honey?"

"Six . . . Seven."

"Henry, Mommy's waiting."

"We've talked enough."

"Henry, please come down and take the phone."

"No!"

Henry let the bags drop one by one. In the silence he heard the sound of footsteps on the stairs echoing the rhythm of his beanbags as they hit the floor.

"Darling, please let me in?" Grandma Martha asked outside his door.

"No."

"What do you want me to tell your mommy?"

"She's not my mommy, she's my mom. And you can tell her I don't want to talk to her."

He was sick of talking or even thinking about his parents, wished that he didn't care so much whether they stayed together or not. But he couldn't help it.

"All right. I'll tell her you'll talk later."

"I don't want to talk to her now or later. Tell her to leave me alone."

As his grandmother retreated down the stairs Henry batted back tears, angry at himself for acting like a baby.

Later, when his dad called, Henry still refused to talk. He was sick of talking to his dad, too. He wouldn't leave his room to eat dinner, either.

"I made your favorite," Grandma Martha said from the hallway. "Fried chicken and mashed potatoes."

"I don't care."

"Henry, please come out and let's talk about what's wrong. It will make you feel better."

"How do you know?"

"Because I used to keep things closed up too. Believe me, that only made things worse."

"My life couldn't get any worse than it is right now."

"Sweetheart, I know you're hurting. I'm hurting too. But things will get better. Now, please, come out. Your dinner is getting cold."

"I'm not coming out. I'm never coming out."

"Henry."

"I don't care if I die in here."

"Please don't talk that way."

"It's true!"

"Henry, you're scaring me."

"Then leave me alone."

"Sweetheart."

Henry threw one of his beanbags at the door.

"What was that?"

"Go away!"

"Henry, open up right now."

When she rattled the doorknob, he began to scream. He kept on screaming until his throat burned. Finally, he lay back on his bed and closed his eyes, taking long, deep breaths on the count of ten to help himself calm down, the way Dr. Cohen had taught him. He was in the middle of his eighteenth deep breath when a familiar deep voice startled him.

"Henry?"

"What?"

"It's Mr. Fine."

"I know."

"Would you please open the door?"

Henry, his eyes still closed, didn't move from his bed. "I don't want to," he said.

"Your grandmother is very upset."

"What can *I* do about it?"

"She wants to see that you're okay."

"If I weren't okay would I be talking to you like this?"

"Henry, I'm serious."

"So am I."

"Your grandma asked me to break down the door."

"Why?"

"She's afraid you might try to hurt yourself."

The thought of Mr. Fine smashing in his door brought Henry off the bed.

"I'm not going to hurt myself."

"Then prove it by opening the door."

"Why should I have to prove it?"

"Because you said something that scared your grandma."

"That's because she's a scaredy-cat. You should see how she treats me. If Grandpa Jay were here, things would be a lot different."

"What you said would have scared him, too."

"No, it wouldn't."

"I knew your grandfather, and I'm sure it would have scared him. The man worshiped the ground you walked on."

Mr. Fine fell silent, as if he was waiting for Henry to say something. *Let him wait,* Henry told himself. But Mr. Fine didn't wait long.

"Henry," he said, "are you going to open up, or do I have to put my shoulder to this door?"

It was no use; the man would not go away.

Unlocking the door, Henry let Mr. Fine usher him downstairs to his grandmother. She welcomed him with a long hug.

"Henry, darling," said Grandma Martha. "I'm sorry that you're so sad and angry."

"I'm not sad or angry. I'm fine. Can't you see?"

Grandma Martha held Henry at arm's length and gazed at him for a long time, as though she were looking at a painting. Henry stared back, willing himself to keep his eyes open without tears.

"I see a boy who's trying very hard to be strong," said his grandmother finally. "A boy his grandpa Jay would be proud of."

"If he were here," said Henry.

"Yes," she said. "If he were here."

"Martha," interrupted Mr. Fine, "I need to get back to Louise now."

"Of course," said Grandma Martha.

She let go of Henry to open the front door for Mr. Fine.

"If you need me again, don't hesitate to call," he said on the way out.

Henry and his grandmother ate dinner without talking much. They watched TV until Grandma Martha fell asleep in her rocking chair. Then Henry tiptoed upstairs to his room and began pulling clothes out of his dresser.

∾ 17 ∾

A PAIR OF JEANS. A GRAY PULLOVER AND A WHITE T-shirt. Two pairs of underwear. Gym socks. Henry's backpack was ready.

The house was dark and quiet when Henry crept down the stairs and slipped past his grandmother, asleep in front of the television. The kitchen clock read ten past eleven. Henry stowed two pieces of fried chicken, a napkin, a bottle of apple juice, and some oatmeal cookies in his backpack and stole out the front door as Grandma Martha snored. He didn't care where he was going; all he wanted was to get away.

Lincoln Street was hushed, except for the crickets, as Henry set off at a brisk pace, but before he had gone a block, bright headlights sent him scurrying for cover behind a privet hedge. A beat-up black convertible stopped across the street from his grandmother's house. Three people got out. In the bright moonlight Henry recognized Carl, Ray, and Willie.

The boys slunk across the street, each clutching something in his hand, but Henry couldn't tell what. He couldn't hear what they were whispering back and forth either.

Henry held very still as the three slipped past his hiding spot and ran down the alley. Ray and Willie headed straight for the Fines' backyard, while Carl paused by Grandma Martha's house. Henry was about to sneak away in the opposite direction when a familiar sound made him pause.

Psssst. Pssssssssst.

It was the hiss of gas escaping from an aerosol can. The moonlight revealed Carl shaking the can in his hand and taking aim at Grandma Martha's house.

Psssst. Psssst. Psssst.

Spray paint streaked across the aluminum siding in long zigzags. Carl shook his can again.

Psssssssssst.

"Hey, guys," Carl whispered loudly. "Check out my masterpiece!"

Psst. Psst. Psssssssssssssssssst.

Henry couldn't ignore it. "Stop that!" he yelled.

The three trespassers froze.

"Who's that?" gasped Willie.

"It's Juggles," hissed Carl.

"Drop those cans!" ordered Henry.

"Shut up, Juggles!"

"I said, drop the cans!"

Carl sprayed the house again. "Make me!"

When Carl pointed the can at him and insolently sprayed paint in his direction, Henry balled his hands into fists and charged.

A light snapped on in the Fines' backyard.

"Someone's coming!" shouted Willie.

Carl waved the paint can. "You want it, Juggles?" he sneered.

The sound of his own feet kicking up the gravel as he ran down the alley toward the boys was the last thing Henry heard before something hard hit his forehead. Then the night turned bright red, and everything stopped.

18

"HENRY?"

A woman was speaking, but Henry couldn't see who it was. The sky was too dark, and she was too far away.

"Sweetheart?"

The voice, closer now, sounded like his mother's. He tried to answer, but his mouth didn't work. He was caught in a dream.

"Henry, sweetheart, come back."

Henry wanted to tell her that he hadn't run away, but the dream wouldn't let him.

"We're right here waiting, pal." That was Dad.

Henry wished the sun would come out so he could see his parents. He wished his mouth would work so he could tell them he was right there. He ached to talk to them.

"We all love you, honey." That was Grandma Martha. "Very, very much."

Her warm kiss on his forehead felt almost real. Henry wished he could talk to her, too.

"Henry"—Mr. Fine's deep voice—"Louise and I have you in our prayers."

Henry wanted to stop dreaming and wake up. *Why can't I?*

"We're all rooting for you, Henry." That was Mom again.

He waited for her to recite another one of her goopy poems. Instead, she said, "Please, Henry, open your eyes."

Henry tried to open his eyes, but he couldn't. He aimed his thoughts in the direction of his mother's voice, but she couldn't hear them. The more she talked, the farther and farther away she got, until her voice faded into silence.

❦ 19 ❧

THEE LIP, THEE LIP.

Henry couldn't tell if the singing bird was part of a dream or not.

Thee lip, thee lip. What-chew, what-chew.

He remembered running down the alley beside his grandmother's house in the dark, but now he could see light through his eyelids. The night was over.

Thee lip, thee lip. What-chew, what-chew, what-chew!

Opening his eyes, Henry saw bunches of flowers lined up around him, like in a florist's shop. Across the room a cardinal perched on a branch outside the window. Except it wasn't his window. And it wasn't his room. Or his bed, either.

"Where?" His mouth felt full of soggy cotton.

"Hello, Henry," someone whispered.

An old man's face came into view above. Grandpa Jay? No, it was someone bigger.

"Mr. Fine?" Henry managed to whisper.

Mr. Fine offered Henry a paper cup with a bent straw in it. "Something to drink?"

Henry nodded and let Mr. Fine help him sit up. Cool water slipped down his throat, sending a delicious shiver all the way to his feet.

"You had us mighty worried."

"Why?"

"You've been unconscious since last night."

"What?"

"Carl Mollenhoffer's spray paint can knocked you out."

Henry touched his forehead and winced as his fingers brushed against a bump the size of his fist. He remembered charging the three boys.

"Did the police catch them?"

"Yes. The two older ones spent the night in juvenile detention and are awaiting trial. I expect they'll be awfully relieved to hear that you've woken up."

"They deserve to stay in jail for a week."

"I'll second that," said Mr. Fine. Gently touching

Henry's shoulder, he added, "I want to thank you for protecting Izzy's Place."

"You're welcome," replied Henry.

Mr. Fine sat in a chair beside the bed.

"That was a noble thing to do, especially considering that I threatened to knock your door down a few hours earlier."

"Would you really have done it?" asked Henry.

Mr. Fine nodded.

"Your grandma was afraid she might lose you. There's only one thing worse than the thought of losing someone you love, and that's actually losing someone you love." Mr. Fine shifted uneasily in his seat. "When I lost Izzy, I thought I'd go crazy."

"How did you lose him?"

"He died of the same blood disease his mother has." Mr. Fine looked down at his hands. "After I found out that I was going to lose Louise, too, I gave up teaching to spend more time with her. Then I built Izzy's Place."

"Why?"

"I needed somewhere to run away to that was close by." Mr. Fine took a handkerchief out of his pocket and blew his nose. "Pretty soon, all I'll have left is that cabin filled with soil samples and memories."

Henry didn't know what to say. Gazing up into Mr. Fine's face, he saw the worry wrinkles that creased his forehead and the sad eyes that asked a question, though he couldn't tell what it was.

"Where's my grandma?" he asked.

"I sent her out with your folks to get some dinner. The three of them were in here all day."

"My mom and dad?"

"They flew in this morning."

Henry tried to swing his legs out of bed.

"Hold your horses, now," said Mr. Fine. "You just woke up."

"But—"

Before Henry could argue, Grandma Martha appeared. As soon as she saw him, her face turned red.

"Henry!" she cried.

"Hi, Grandma."

"Oh, Henry, darling!"

She kissed him and held her cheek against his for a long time. Henry felt tears on his skin.

"I'm okay, Grandma," he assured her. "Really."

"I know." She kept on hugging him. "It's just that I'm so relieved to see you awake."

Moments later, Henry's parents hurried in, followed quickly by a stream of doctors and nurses. Before Henry knew it, the room was filled with people, all of them smiling and wishing him well. He didn't notice Mr. Fine slip away in all the excitement.

20

THEY LET HENRY LEAVE THE HOSPITAL THE NEXT DAY after lunch. His mother and grandmother sat on either side of him in the backseat and held his hands while his dad drove Grandma Martha's station wagon. His parents helped him up the front steps of the house, holding him under the arms like he was made of porcelain.

"I'm okay," he insisted.

"We know," said his dad.

"We want to help you anyway," said his mom.

They lounged lazily on blankets and pillows in

the backyard for the rest of the day, eating ice-cream sundaes and playing checkers. Henry gave a juggling demonstration, even though his head still hurt a little. By eight o'clock Grandma Martha was so worn out from the previous days' excitement that she tottered off to bed. But Henry's parents wouldn't leave his side. His mom even followed him into the bathroom and watched him brush his teeth.

"Mom?" said Henry finally.

"What, sweetheart?"

"Could I have some privacy?"

She smiled sheepishly and left him alone after that, but she and his dad were waiting for him in his room when he got out. After Henry slipped into bed, his dad read from a book he had bought for him in the airport. It was a story about a family who drinks water from a magical spring that gives them eternal life. But rather than live happily ever after, the family is sad, because they can't die. They know that life is supposed to be like a wheel that keeps turning, that plants, animals, and people are supposed to keep falling off while new ones keep jumping on. One mustn't stop the wheel. Things have to grow and change. That's the way life is supposed to be. Dying is part of it.

Henry saw how still his mother sat as his father read the story. *She's probably thinking about*

Grandpa Jay, he thought, and hoped the book helped her feel better.

He wondered if Mr. Fine might like to read the book if he hadn't heard of it before. He'd have to ask him the next time they saw each other.

When his dad finished reading, his mom turned off the light, but his parents remained in the room.

"We've been talking," said his dad.

"About what?" Henry asked.

"About you."

"We thought you might want to come home with us," said his mom.

"Why?"

"What do you mean, why?"

"I thought you and Dr. Cohen thought it would be better for me to stay here?"

"We did, but if you're so unhappy here with Grandma Martha, it defeats the purpose."

"It wasn't because of her. I was unhappy at home, too."

His mother gathered him in her arms and hugged him tight. "Henry, Henry," she murmured.

"Does this mean you want to stay here?" asked his dad.

"I don't know. The house isn't the same without Grandpa Jay."

No one said anything for a while.

"Let's sleep on it," said his mother finally. "And we can talk it over tomorrow. Okay?"

"Okay," said Henry.

Then they both kissed him good night and left the room.

∽ 21 ∾

GRANDMA MARTHA HAD ALREADY LEFT FOR WORK BY the time Henry woke up and wandered downstairs. He found his parents together in the kitchen. It was a relief to hear them talking easily to each other. A wonderful smell filled the air. Banana pancakes, his dad's breakfast specialty, were cooking on the stove. Their aroma reminded Henry of good times at home.

"I hope you're hungry," said his dad.

"Starving," said Henry.

His mom served him a huge stack of the silver dollar–size pancakes. He bathed them in maple syrup and dug in.

"Well?" asked his dad as Henry swallowed his first bite.

"Best food I've eaten since I left New Jersey," he said.

His mom laughed as he stuffed himself, then pointed to a freshly baked pie sitting on the counter.

"Mr. Fine dropped that off while you were sleeping." She handed him an envelope. "This came with it."

The envelope had Henry's name neatly printed in pen across it. Inside there was a card with a picture of a scientist holding a test tube on the front. Opening the card, Henry found a short message:

Here's hoping this special formula helps you get back on your feet fast.

> *Your friends,*
> *Ernie and Louise Fine*

The pie was blueberry. Henry showed his parents the card. They both smiled, even though they didn't understand what the whole thing really meant.

Henry and his family drove to the airport the next day. The cornstalks seemed to wave at them in the breeze as they passed, and the ride went quickly. Henry decided those were signs that meant he had made the right decision. There was nothing he could do for his parents; whether or not they stayed together was beyond his control. Like Grandma Martha said, the best he could do was not give up.

It was a long way through the terminal. His injured forehead throbbed by the time they got to the gate. His mom brushed a strand of hair from his eyes.

"Well," she said, "the plane is waiting."

"I know," Henry replied.

"Are you sure about this?" asked his dad.

"Yep," he said, though in another minute he was afraid he might change his mind.

His mom looked at Grandma Martha. "Enjoy yourselves."

Grandma Martha smiled at Henry. "We will."

He took her hand.

"Good luck with summer school," he said to his mother.

"Thanks," she said.

"Don't work too hard, Dad," Henry said.

"Okay, champ."

They shook hands and hugged. Then his mom hugged him and Grandma Martha and walked with Henry's dad through the gate.

After they got back from the airport and had lunch, Henry told Grandma Martha to go to work.

"What about you?" she asked.

"I'll be okay here," he said.

"Won't you be lonely?"

"Nah."

Grandma Martha didn't argue. Hugging him gently, she said, "It's good to have you here."

"It's good to be here." He hugged her back tightly.

After his grandmother left, Henry crossed to the fireplace and reached for the deck of playing cards on the mantel beside Grandpa Jay's pipe. He put the pack in his pocket and went outside.

The giant sycamore swayed gently in the breeze, its leaves whispering some secret message, while the rickety swing rocked back and forth, as if powered by an invisible child. As Henry strode across the lawn to his neighbors' yard, a blue jay swooped out of the towering tree and scolded him for invading its territory. Henry kept going.

The strains of sweet violin music beckoned from Izzy's Place. Henry didn't know what would happen when he returned home, but for now, he decided it was up to him to make the best of things while he was here. Wondering if Mr. Fine knew how to play Go Fish or gin rummy, he knocked once on the cabin door and entered as soon as it opened.